An Anthology
of
Witty
&
Oddball
Village Stories

An Anthology
of
Witty
&
Oddball
Village Stories

Alan L. Simons

BARONEL BOOKS
Toronto, Canada.

This edition is published by Baronel Books, Toronto, Canada.

First Paperback Edition 2025

Alan L. Simons asserts the moral right to be identified as the author of this work.

This work is a fictional embellishment.

Names, characters, places, and incidents are products of the author's vivid imagination and are not construed as real. Any resemblance to actual events, locales, or persons, living or dead, is entirely coincidental and possibly due to the reader's vivid imagination.

Library and Archives Canada Cataloguing in Publication information is available upon request.

ISBN: 978-1-7782137-6-2

https://anthologystories.me

anthologystories@proton.me

baronelbooks.com

DEDICATION

I thank my wonderful family and friends, who continue, even today, to have an inordinate amount of patience to put up with my unique sense of satire, humour, and style. Why? I've yet to understand.

As the late American Hugh Swanson Sidey, White House historian and veteran writer, famed for his book *Portraits of the Presidents* once said: "A sense of humour... is needed armour. Joy in one's heart and some laughter on one's lips is a sign that the person down deep has a pretty good grasp of life."

Hugh, as I will briefly call him, died in 2005. Such a pity he didn't live for at least another twenty years.

ACKNOWLEDGMENTS

"J", I gratefully acknowledge you for your support and constructive advice in the characterisations mentioned in this book.

Shamelessly, I have used several quotes taken from numerous sources, including *BrainyQuote,* an online resource medium.

CONTENTS

Prologue: Village Stories for Like-Minded Friends

Prologue

Village Stories for Like-Minded Friends

Dear Friends,

Many years ago, three distinct communities from Newfoundland and Labrador, Wales, and Eastern Europe, each found their way to southeastern France. They happily established themselves exclusively in their own concealed worlds, without a care or a familiarity with their surroundings. That is until a stranger of senior years had the tenacity to venture forth on a path to document more of what had been little written about them. I acknowledge to you from the outset that I am that stranger.

After an extensive period of research, I won't bore you with the details, but in all fairness to you, a clue at this time to their salubrious locations might be meaningful. I established that the three communities, the villages of Little Figgy-on-the-Duff, Little Pletzl-on-the-Zump, and Little Comely-on-the-Marsh, are located southwest of Route D61, the forests of Commune d'Establet and the Ruisseau d'Establet in the department of Drôme.

I'm sure you may know the area from your bike tours, or perhaps you have hiked in the region while observing the occasional French farmer milking his Montbéliarde.

My journey first starts in the village of Little Figgy-on-the-Duff. The village is a distinct, proud, and homogeneous community from Newfoundland and Labrador, whose ancestors originally fled to southeastern France because of a fear that the Vikings would make them wear traditional Norse clothing and take over the dry salt cod industry.

As any traveller of habit will tell you, Newfoundlanders and Labradorians, above all, are the friendliest people you can come across anywhere. One of the joys of the residents is telling you stories about their ancestors.

And with that, I shall now begin.

-Alan L. Simons, Toronto, 2025

"I will never regret getting old.
I know too many people who have never had that
privilege."

CHAPTER ONE

The Little Figgy Music Ensemble
Or, shitbaked has nothing to do with pie

Tell me now, what would a village containing an abundance of Newfoundland and Labrador roots be without a gathering of melophiles? Little Figgy, in that respect, is no different from other small communities. However, I acknowledge that their taste might seem a little, shall we say, unique, but generally speaking, their adoration for music covers a whole eclectic selection of interests.

The Little Figgy Music Ensemble, commonly known locally as the Little Figgy Quintet, as I will now call them, consists of a group of five diehards who meet every Thursday evening, at seven and a half past the hour, at the Little Figgy Community Centre. Their music, for the most part, includes Newfoundland and Labrador sea shanties and sailing songs from a long time ago.

Their superb musical director, composer, and arranger is hymnodist Delbert Brown. You may know of him. He is also chair of the Little Figgy Music Circle, famed for its hymn melodies. If there's one hymn that sticks in everyone's mind, I'm sure you are familiar with it, it is the rendering of the well-known version of, *It is not good for a man to be alone*, arranged for music of course in the baroque style by Delbert Brown, with lyrics by our Father John Murphy.

It is told in some quarters that at the time of writing, I cannot collaborate, that Delbert's ancestors were acquainted with the English composer Henry Purcell.

The quintet's musical instruments, as one would expect, include the bodhrán, the ugly stick, the accordion, and the fiddle. Mayor Sadie Parsons plays the bodhrán. Her husband, Jack Parsons, is the fiddler. Chief Constable Gabriel White plays the ugly stick, and the widow Murphy is on the accordion. Occasionally, if appropriate, the musical saw is introduced, also played remarkably well by the widow Murphy.

Mrs Blanche White is the quintet's lead singer. She has sung for most of her three score and fifteen years, habitually out of tune. But she does have a lovely personality, as well as making a delicious spicy partridgeberry cake.

It was the Thursday one month before the annual Little Figgy Hootie Music Festival. All of the quintet's members were told in advance to arrive early for their weekly rehearsal. Delbert Brown had some news he wanted to share with the group.

"I'm delighted to tell you," he said with a smile on his face that acknowledged something of importance was going to happen. "I'm delighted to tell you that this year our Music Festival has a sponsor." He paused, waiting for the oohing and ahhing from those present. He wasn't disappointed. "Yes, our very own village church, the Gates of Heaven Help Us, has agreed to sponsor our humble quintet to celebrate the birthday of Saint Fiacre, the patron saint for haemorrhoid sufferers."

Delbert paused once more to take in the thrill of what is expected from a hymnodist.

"I'm also excited to inform you that this year we will be performing two new sailing songs." He paused again to express the full effect of his next eleven words. "Which I have written and set to music for you all."

Mrs Blanche White let out one of her delightful, timely screams, which in itself was unusual since she was always customarily late for rehearsals.

Delbert favourably acknowledged the scream with a nod of his head. He continued.

"The two compositions are called *Love is Sweet, but it's Tastier with a Piece of Fish* and *I'm a Son of a Sea Cook*."

He turned to face Mrs Blanche White.

"Blanche, will you flavour us by singing *Love is Sweet, but it's Tastier with a Piece of Fish*?"

Without waiting too long for an appropriate acknowledgement from his lead singer, he turned to face his quintet.

"And as a special honour, Jötunn White, Little Figgy's baker, butcher, veterinary pathologist, and if I might add, primo uomo singer in the sea shanties and sailing songs category, has agreed to join us to sing, *I'm a Son of a Sea Cook*."

Without exception, all those present were in rapturous harmony, as I was, with the news.

"And now", said Delbert, "Here are the lead sheets for each of you. Let's have a run-through. We only have a month to get into shape."

All the rehearsals, leading up to the annual Little Figgy Hootie Music Festival, were remarkably good, that is, up to a point. I have no notion how it happened other than to say that Mrs Blanche White, in one of her enthusiastic moments, a few days before the opening event, presented each member of the quintet with their very own homemade spicy partridgeberry pie.

Perhaps it was the molasses or spices, or as the village doctor, Dr Piddy Adfat, confided in me, perhaps it was the toothpicks inserted and accidentally left in the pies that most likely caused everyone to react to their digestive system.

At the time, I can tell you, Delbert was shitbaked! But, be as it may, all members of the quintet recovered sufficiently to proudly perform in the music festival.

As for Mrs Blanche White? She admitted her rendering of *Love is Sweet but it's Tastier with a Piece of Fish* bore no resemblance to her spicy partridgeberry pies.

And for that, we are all truly thankful. Amen.

.

"There were 15 people in the village, including five of us. If my father arrested somebody in the winter, he'd have to wait until the thaw to turn him in."

-Leslie Nielsen

CHAPTER TWO

Know your buts from your Butts and Bobbers

If there is one sports event that receives much enthusiastic acclaim from the villagers of Little Figgy, it is the summer solstice's annual Piddly Sports Competition, called by the acronym PIST.

PIST is held on the grounds of the Little Figgy Duff Playing Field. To give credit where credit's due, the field is superbly maintained by Wayne Brown-White. He's their noteworthy Athletic Turf Manager and Entomologist.

Much to the sheer delight of our Father John Murphy, of the Church of Gates of Heaven Help Us, this sports event, in the time-honoured tradition, is in celebration of England granting religious freedom to Roman Catholics in Newfoundland in 1794.

Recently, some of the seniors in the village have added Tipsy to the name Piddly Sports

Competition, in tribute to our Father Murphy for his philanthropic services to Little Figgy, including his offering of a round of drinks, at twelve and a half o'clock, to all the patrons of Chummy's Pub, in honour of this annual celebratious occasion.

And outside of Chummy's Pub, on this day, at the deepest edge of the Figgy Pond, there's a large handwritten sign with a well-defined arrow pointing downward. "No personal butt caps or handles allowed in the pub. Leave your butt here!" The term butt, I will tell you, is understood by all you anglers out there. For the rest of us, bear with me a minute!

In Chummy's, much about the traditional game of Butt was being discussed by a group led by the villager's sports psychohistorian, Tanith Immilla Walsh.

As explained by Tanith Immilla Walsh, while her partner Wayne Brown-White looked on in admiration, the game of Butt hadn't changed over the ensuing years in Little Figgy's society's sports culture. Originally, years ago, it was established by Little Figgy's avid fishermen, all over the age of 70 years, who needed something to keep them socially and cognitively engaged.

"Besides spending our time talking about the old times and drinking beer, we need to create a game to challenge our physical and mental state," piped up one old-timer. "But, perhaps a ball game based on fishing?" another one added.

And that is how the game of Butt started. Today, it stands as the village's quintessential community sports game for mature seniors and is an integral part of life for many of Little Figgy's citizens. Playing Butt fulfils their lonely life admirably.

But, Butt has also another name. The villagers' anglers call it "The Fisherman's Game." It is a game requiring utter concentration, mental energy, and the ability to avoid accusatory language, of which the latter for Little Figgy's seniors causes them to have insurmountable challenges.

For those of you who aren't too familiar with playing Butt, I shall now attempt to introduce to you the basic rules of the game, played on a field of no definitive size.

The game is played between two opposing teams of five players. Each player, while on the Duff Playing Field, must be over the age of 70 years. Their height and weight are irrelevant. So is their gender.

Simply put, to play Butt, the equipment one needs includes one butt cap attached to a handle, plus four butts, and one fisherman's bobber. One places the four butts upright in the ground, five cm apart, behind the hitter.

For those of you who are acquainted with the game of cricket, you might so far see some familiarity with Butt. But that's where the familiarity ends.

As tradition dictates, during the game, both the hitter and the thrower each wear the following outfits at all times, fishing gloves, hip waders, and a sou'wester hat. One's colour is of choice.

The game is played by a team player taking one turn each throwing the bobber in an attempt to knock down any or all of the four butts. If the hitter hits the bobber, the hitter gets one point. If the thrower catches the bobber hit by the hitter, his team gets five points and a pint of Little Figgy beer paid for by the opposing side. But, and this is where it gets so interesting, if the thrower knocks down any or all of the four butts by the hitter missing hitting the bobber, the hitter is out of the game.

Finally, if by throwing the bobber the thrower hits the hitter either by accident or on purpose, Little Figgy's chief constable, Gabriel White, and his dog Goobies have to call in reinforcements to separate the two teams.

And there you have it, the game of Butt! If Newfoundland and Labrador is on your bucket list, make sure you know the difference between your buts from your butts and bobbers.

CHAPTER THREE

Jim, the School Crossing Guard and stand-up weekend comedian at Chummy's Pub

Politics aside, I have thoroughly investigated the whys and wherefores of the employment of a school crossing guard in the village of Little Figgy. It would seem years ago, if I remember - you can correct me if I am mistaken - the village's Council had a vision to establish a safety review committee to determine safety standards for students.

In due course, they appointed a select committee, called Figgy Action Committee for a Children's Safe Environment (FACFACSE). The objective was to contribute, through discussion, to a healthy village by encouraging walking to school and ensuring walking routes are safe.

After months of deliberation and countless meetings, FACFACSE concluded their outcome would be pointless without retaining a school crossing guard.

If you have the slightest reservations about what may be behind the FACFACSE conclusion, well, I have to tell you there's a story about to be told.

I am sure most of us of a certain age will remember our school crossing guards. Some of us may even remember their names. I do not! I do remember they looked ancient. They seemed to appear and disappear into oblivion during certain times of day, only to return the next school morning, thirty minutes before school began and thirty minutes before school ended.

I want to share this remarkable and fascinating moment in memorabilia with you as my method of introducing you to Little Figgy's only school crossing guard.

His name is Liol White-Walsh-Parsons. He's also a stand-up comedian and former politician. He goes by the stage name of "Jim", and that is what I will call him from now on. Indeed, you would be justified in questioning why the village needs a school crossing guard all decked out in uniform and a hand-held STOP sign.

I will tell you that the fundamental trouble I have with all of this is that the village is devoid of any motorized vehicles. There are no highways, arteries, main or public roads, streets, bicycle lanes, or wot not, for children or adults to cross. The village's primary means of getting from A to

B is by taking one of the handful of walking paths, none of which have been designated by any name.

Now, I will also tell you there was a time some years ago, that the Little Figgy Council Cabinet had arbitrarily voted, during one of their Monday lunches and liquid refreshments at Mudders Restaurant, to naming the Little Figgy walking paths and lanes with such names as Ticklemeallover, DildoDrums, and Blowmedown, all I might add in remembrance and respect to the original inhabitants of the Little Figgy community dating back hundreds of years ago.

And this is where it gets so intriguing. Such a suggestion got back to Figgy's only medical doctor, Dr Piddy Adfat, and her husband, Baba Younus, who were most distressed. They insisted there was also a value in remembering their distant family past. It was, to put it into perspective, to make Figgy great again.

Well, Little Figgy's Cabinet Council discussed it at length at their Monday lunch. Present were Mayor Sadie Parsons, Deputy Mayor Lisa Walsh, the Executive Committee members led by our Father John Murphy, Zebedee Parsons, Enosh Walsh-White, and Business Manager Annie White-Brown. Dr Piddy Adfat had sent her regrets. One of her beloved peacocks was suffering from an endoparasitic infection. All those present were deeply affected and sent their best wishes for a speedy recovery to Dr Piddy.

However, as many of the council members had

their annual medical check-ups coming up, they flip-flopped on their previous decision and agreed unanimously to the doctor's request.

Unfortunately, as they found out after the good doctor had submitted her suggested names, they were either unpronounceable, false, or the names were far too long.

I will continue. The Little Figgy Cabinet Council, the Little Figgy Action Committee for a Children's Safe Environment (FACFACSE), Jim the Crossing Guard, and Dr Piddy Adfat and her husband Baba Younus searched in vain for a compromise.

Indeed, the compromise, or I should say a suggestion came from Jim, who was not only wearing a sleeveless red shirt with the words 'I'm Jim the Crossing Guard' proudly emblazoned on the back, but also fluorescent yellow shorts, and hiking boots. He said, "Why not ask Yitzhak, the stranger amongst us, for his opinion?"

It was Enosh White-Walsh, the village's legal officer, who reacted. "Jim, get out of here, you little sleeveen. I dies for you, but this ain't Friday night comedy hour at Chummy's!" The doctor and her husband, Baba Younus, with a nod of their heads gave their enthusiastic support to Enosh's comment.

Jim, being the artiste that he is, slowly stood up, raised his crossing guard STOP sign high above his head while twirling it around, and turning towards Mayor Sophie Parsons cried out,

"I resign! I resign!" And with a flurry of theatrical emotion, he started to sing *Remember Me* from Purcell's Dido's Lament, as he walked unhurriedly away from the Little Figgy Council Chambers, down the hill, accompanied by a pair of white wagtails intently listening to him, as their long white-sided tails moved up and down conjointly to the melody.

"Jaysus!" remarked Mayor Parsons. "I had no idea he could sing! That brought tears to me eyes!"

En route home, Jim, now with an appetite from his rendering of *Remember Me*, stopped at Burbots Fish and Chips Shop where, with his STOP sign still in his right hand, he ordered a special large portion of crispy potato fries, with the ends cut off, which he shared with the white wagtails.

A short time later, the Little Figgy Cabinet Council flipped-flopped and discharged the select committee called Figgy Action Committee for a Children's Safe Environment (FACFACSE) of its appointed task by rescinding the motion that originally established it.

Speaking to me about what happened, Mayor Sadie Parsons stated she had now discharged FACFACSE because of over-involvement by the committee and the change they wanted to initiate into the village's traditional way of life. More importantly, she was deeply saddened that Jim had refused to hand in his right-hand-held STOP sign, the only one in existence.

"I always check with elders back in the village before I try out something new."

- Chef Damu

CHAPTER FOUR

When Love Conquers All

Especially during times of political disorder, if there's nothing more that connects a reader to a story, it is a tale of love, romance, and intrigue. And that is what is about to happen.

I will call it, "The romantic journey between Nurse Tryphena of the Little Figgy Medical Centre and Rodney Parsons, the co-manager of Tea & Teeth, Little Figgy's Co-op Grocery Store."

Nurse Tryphena, RPN (Registered Psychiatric Nurse), suffers from Body Dysmorphic Disorder (BDD). She spends an inordinate amount of time worrying about imperfections in her appearance. Sadly her dream to follow in the footsteps of Charmion, the famous trapeze artiste and strongwoman, came to an abrupt end when her GP, Dr Piddy Adfat, suggested an excessive period hanging upside down, as many dance trapeze artists do, might result in an increase in blood pressure to her eyes that may damage them.

Nurse Tryphena was devastated. However, her friend Rodney Parsons continued to give her the emotional support befitting of someone in his position. Their marriage followed. Our Father John Murphy, of the Gates of Heaven Help Us, officiated, and their friend the stranger Yitzhak, as expected of him, gave a warm toast to the bride and groom, followed by, "Let's eat!"

The couple took up residence in a lovely two-bedroom house, painted in the colours of white, blue, red, and gold, located on the west side of the Little Figgy village pond, just behind the Little Figgy Co-op Grocery Store and Jötunn and Lisa White's Little Figgy bakery and butcher store.

Surrounding their house, the married couple planted a profusion of Sarracenia purpurea L. You would, I'm sure, obviously know it as the insect-eating pitcher plant, a plant not at all appreciated by the local village arachnids.

Tryphena and Rodney were inseparable. So it seemed! However, a few months into their marriage and on the insistence of his wife, Rodney visited Dr Piddy Adfat. She diagnosed Rodney with a rare condition called philematophobia, an extreme fear of kissing.

Dr Piddy Adfat's diagnosis took on a whole new meaning for the couple. Their marriage vows were in disarray. Rodney, before his marriage, was a sort of quiet chap who took his role in life very seriously in growing organic fruits and vegetables, running workshop classes, and with his friend, the entomologist Wayne White, he would organize group walks within the forest discussing the ability of various insects to track odours to their sources. He had, if I can put it to you, the makings of becoming one of Little Figgy's few accomplished ordinary beings.

But now? He had become very distant. He had almost given up helping his twin brother Terry with running the Tea & Teeth Co-op Store, preferring to take solitary walks in the forest, while observing the birdish antics of the Eurasian Griffon, and on some days, even the Little Ringed Plover.

And what of Nurse Tryphena? As recommended by Dr Piddy Adfat, based on her health inhibiting her work performance, she took time off from the Little Figgy Medical Centre. Tryphena's twin sister, Nurse Tryphosa RN, being as they say of sound mind, was quite capable of standing in for her.

Tryphena, in the meantime, returned to her dad's restaurant, Jigs Diner, helping him out the best she could, serving the customers but always talking about her love lost opportunity of becoming a dance trapeze artiste.

Today, as you enter Jigs Diner, if you glance up towards the far end, by the window, facing the church The Gates of Heaven Help Us, you will see hanging on the wall, a short pre-taped horizontal bar dangling from two ropes, and a one-piece leotard handmade costume in stretched velvet, crystal-embellished and magnificently hand-painted throughout. Below the costume is a framed photo of Albert Einstein with the words, "You can't blame gravity for falling in love."

CHAPTER FIVE

A Classic Easter Story: The Case of the Mudders Maundy Thursday Baked Mug Cakes
Or, why did Izan, the pet peacock, have to die?

Part One

Friends, whatever you may have heard about the origins of the iconic Mug Cakes, you should immediately put your mind to rest! I can honestly say, with the utmost authority, that they are all fables of numerous gastronomists brought on by their desire to show their Easter heritage of this tantalizing and scrumptious food, known for hundreds of years as the stable comfort dessert.

Having said that, I can claim from talking with many of my present-day acquaintances in Newfoundland and Labrador that it was Mrs

Violet White-Walsh, the Michelin chef supreme of the Mudders Restaurant, in the village of Little Figgy-on-the-Duff, who can attest to all that I now will tell you.

For many generations, as the tale dictates, it was the wife of Captain William Whittle of Whittle's Bay, Newfoundland, who left the secret ingredients to the residents of Whittle's Bay. When Captain Whittle died, his widow and her children returned to England. As a gesture of thanks and friendship to Mrs Whittle, the village community changed the name of the village to Whittles-less Bay. Eventually, it became known as Witless Bay.

Now, this is where it gets interesting: Mrs Violet White-Walsh, from her earliest days, dreamed of being a pâtissière. Mrs White-Walsh, or as she was known at the time by her maiden name, Violet White, was a colourful person who separated from Will Walsh early in their marriage, just after their daughter Rosie was born. The details are immaterial to this tale.

Sadly, Will Walsh, or as he became known by his nickname, "Won't Walsh", died at the age of 23 during the winter solstice from seasonal affective disorder, exactly on the day of his birthday, as he sat there in loneliness, blowing out his solitary birthday candle.

Violet, an assiduous character, with the help of her mother, brought up her daughter Rosie and opened up a small restaurant called Mudders. Located on the sunny side of the Little Figgy Pond, between Dr Piddy Adfat's Medical Centre and The Little Figgy Community Centre, Mudders became an instant success, especially for its superb desserts, including during Easter, the iconic Maundy Thursday Baked Mug Cake.

But Violet's insistence on calling herself a pâtissière wretchedly affected her walk-in trade. None of her clients could correctly pronounce 'pâtissière.' So, eventually, Violet resigned herself, with the greatest of effort, to simply calling herself a pastry chef.

And now this is where we are today, the Thursday morning before Good Friday.

Our Father Murphy, of the Gates of Heaven Help Us, as was the Little Figgy custom, read out the traditional five-word Mudders Maundy Thursday Baked Mug Cakes short prayer to pastry chef Violet, as she commenced on her journey to complete her deliverance, much to the appreciation of all those present.

"Stir up, we beseech thee."

One could say, and I will, that the prayer was similar to a starting pistol used at sports events. It gave Violet White-Walsh carte blanche authority to start preparing her Mudders Maundy Thursday Baked Mug Cakes containing her celebrated and secret ingredient.

As she so articulately expressed quietly to me

and in confidence, "Fruit. Yes, peach, blueberry, and apple are a must. So is honey, pumpkin, and strawberries, along with my secret ingredient."

She looked at me with a wicked grin. "I suppose it wouldn't hurt to tell you, would it? For a wild and robust aroma, I add some tuber melanosporum. You know them as black truffles. I picked them myself last night." She paused, took a long breath, and said with a straight face, "And I also complement it with lots of Little Figgy's 60% alcohol-proof brandy. It's aged at least 10 years in oak. Fit for the Lord this Easter, I say! Amen!"

She added, "Indispensable, isn't it? Here, you must taste it, neat!"

Indeed! I relished the opportunity. I was not disappointed.

Perhaps it was just as well our Father John Murphy wasn't in the vicinity. He was still struggling with Dr Piddy Adfat's diagnosis of him having a saccadic nystagmus condition.

Violet continued. "After it's cooked..." she proudly pointed to a dark storage location at the back of her Mudders kitchen, where already hundreds of Mudders Maundy Thursday Baked Mug Cakes ordered for the eventual day sat quietly in their glory.

I am now preparing you for the worst.

To quote the great Chinese philosopher of Confucianism, Xun Kuang, who has nothing personally to do with this story, he said: "Pride and excess bring disaster to man."

And so it also did for Chef Violet White-Walsh. Disaster struck the next morning, during the early hours of Good Friday, sometime before nautical twilight.

If I could raise some absurd humour at the incident, the proverb "the early bird catches the worm" comes to mind.

It was our Father John Murphy who first raised the alarm. On his Good Friday early morning stroll, past the Little Figgy Duff University and the Little Figgy Community Centre towards Mudders Restaurant, he stopped and took a deep breath to smell the lavender, thyme, and rosemary. He also took the time to observe the prickly juniper and plethora of evergreen shrubs, as well as notice with curiosity, a muster of intoxicated peacocks and peahens staggering happily back to their pen as fast as their ugly legs could take them, with helpings of Maundy Thursday Baked Mug Cakes on their beaks and feathers!

Violet, who while arriving early to prepare her orders for delivery, let out a scream that was heard throughout the village.

Witnessing the scene of destruction with Violet, our Father John Murphy could think of only one heart-wrenching thing to say to her as they both looked at the storage site consisting now only of small vestiges of baked Mug Cakes.

"Violet," he said with a sorrowful look on his

face, "As it is written in John 6:12, Gather up the fragments that remain, that nothing be lost."

Upon hearing those scriptural words, Violet let out a further piercing scream of such a high pitch that one of the sozzled peacocks walking in circles nearby, smelling of Little Figgy's 60% alcohol-proof brandy, looked up at her, made a loud screech, rolled over, and fell dead!

It was Mayor Sadie Parsons, accompanied by Chief Constable Gabriel White and his dog, Goobies, who were next to arrive at the scene of the catastrophe, followed by Dr Piddy Adfat and her husband, Baba Younus.

On observing the scene, the doctor became utterly distraught. "What have you done to my precious pet Izan? He was the leader of his muster and my pride and joy. He loved his little peachicks!"

"Yes, he certainly loved his little peachicks. No doubt about it!" added Baba Younus, as all of those present encircled precious Izan.

"Your precious Izan? YOUR PRECIOUS IZAN?" (I add the capitals to emphasize Violet's tone of voice).

"What about all my Mudders Maundy Thursday Baked Mug Cakes? It's a disaster! All of them are eaten by your peacocks and peahens. ALL OF THEM! You're cracked!" To which Dr Piddy Adfat sarcastically replied, whispering in her fashionable way, "Yes, Wad-a-Piddy!"

"Yes, Wad-a-Piddy!" added Baba Younus, in

support of his wife, as he looked behind him at the stranger approaching.

"Ay, what's after happening now?" It was the stranger Yitzhak. Mayor Sadie Parsons pointed down at precious Izan.

"How's he getting on?" responded Yitzhak.

"With difficulty! He's dead!" replied the Mayor.

"Dead?" exclaimed Yitzhak.

"Yes, dead!" remarked our Father Murphy.

I briefly pause to express the full benefit of you hearing the articulate, exhilarating dialogue now being spoken by all those present.

"Sometime overnight, he..." Violet pointed at Izan, "he brought all his peacocks and peahens up here." She gestured to the open door at the side of her Mudders Restaurant. "They went in, I don't know how, and they started to eat my Mudders Maundy Thursday Baked Mug Cakes, the ones ordered for Good Friday delivery."

"And you," pointed Dr Piddy Adfat towards Violet White-Walsh, "You, you let them in. My gorgeous pet peacocks and peahens! My darling Izan."

"He's dead!" added Yitzhak.

"Yes, we know that!" butted in our Father Murphy.

Yitzhak turned to the doctor. "Are you going to say a prayer for Izan?"

"A prayer?" replied Dr Piddy Adfat. "A PRAYER? No, we shall have a full traditional funeral ceremony. The whole thing for my darling Izan! Today!"

Our Father Murphy cautiously stepped forward as if to say something.

"Our Father Murphy, please, will you be the officiant?" asked the doctor.

I must say, I have no personal knowledge of a Roman Catholic priest officiating at the funeral of a pet peacock, and certainly, not a drunk peacock who was the leader of his muster with the name of Izan.

However, our Father Murphy, being a trooper as he is, generously agreed to be the officiant.

Baba Younus spoke up. "We'll take Izan back to our parlour and await instructions from ..."

"Hold your horses right now!" Mayor Sophie Parsons stepped forward. "There be no pet peacock-picking-whatsoever funeral service for Izan until we have a post-mortem. We have to determine the cause of death. I'll speak to Jötunn White, he's our butcher as well as our veterinary pathologist."

"How about death by stuffing himself while eating my Mudders Maundy Thursday Baked Mug Cakes?" remarked Violet White-Walsh.

"Yes, that sounds reasonable," said Yitzhak, looking at Violet with a twinkle in his left eye.

"Now, now! This has nothing to do with you! You're a stranger to these parts," replied the Mayor.

Our Father Murphy immediately saw the

opportunity to do what men of his stature do best. He intervened, crossed himself, and looked at them one by one, quoting from his bible. "Be at peace with each other. Mark 9:50."

Part Two

The next day, Mayor Sadie Parsons convened an emergency meeting of the Little Figgy Council's Cabinet to deal with the death of Izan, the pet peacock.

Typically, over Easter, it was the period for the villagers to spend time with their loved ones, but as Mayor Parsons told her husband, "I intend to work right through these issues so that we can immediately tackle this crisis head-on. This is a pressing matter that can't wait. We're all Figgys here, and it's Easter. Elbows up!"

The emergency meeting was held in camera the following afternoon, at one thirty. Those in attendance included Mayor Sadie Parsons, Deputy Mayor Lisa Walsh, and the executive committee. Allyship: Father Murphy; Health: Piddy Adfat, MD; Agriculture and Environment: Zebedee Parsons; Legal: Enosh White-Walsh, and Business Manager Annie White-Brown.

The meeting didn't start very well.

"Mayor Parsons." Enosh White-Walsh, in his capacity as 'Legal,' arose and cleared his throat.

"I ask that Dr Adfat recuse herself from this

meeting. If I may quote an old mid-century proverb by William Turner," he turned to face Dr Adfat.

"By association and out of respect to you, I quote the well-known saying, 'Byrdes of on kynde and colour flok and flye allwayes together.'"

Dr Piddy Adfat, not known at any time for being at a loss for words, sat there in shock and I admit if I had any knowledge of medicine I would have to say her jaw muscles became so tight I wondered if she had acquired a condition called Trismus, muscle spasms in her, yes you are correct, her temporomandibular joint.

Enosh White-Walsh didn't waste any further time. He continued.

"Mayor Parsons. I understand one of Dr Adfat's prize pet peacocks allegedly got loose and with the assistance of his muster, they entered, without permission, the premises known as Mudders Restaurant and took a fancy to Mrs White-Walsh's delicious Mudders Maundy Thursday Baked Mug Cakes. The Mug Cakes, I am led to believe, were awaiting delivery that morning, to numerous households in Little Figgy."

"And all paid for in advance," remarked Business Manager, Annie White-Brown.

"Thank you, Annie. Thank you for that important detail. Yes, all paid for in advance!" responded Enosh White-Walsh.

The Mayor raised her hand. "You have a point. I agree, we do have a competing interest here in front of us." The Mayor turned toward Dr Piddy Adfat.

"Dr Adfat, in a few minutes our veterinary pathologist, Jötunn White, will advise us on what his findings are from the post-mortem of Izan, the peacock, which was your pet peacock. Kindly recuse yourself."

At this point in my story, I have to explain that my knowledge of local Little Figgy-on-the-Duff bylaws leaves much to be desired. However, I will say Dr Adfat, after much consternation and facial expressions, did recuse herself.

"Jötunn White, please advise us of your findings in this matter."

Jötunn White, Little Figgy's veterinarian pathologist, butcher on Tuesdays, Thursdays, and Saturdays, a baker on Mondays, Wednesdays, and Fridays, and primo uomo singer in the sea shanties and sailing songs category, acknowledged all the village cabinet council members present.

"Thank you, Mayor Parsons. Yes, my findings regarding the post-mortem of the pet peacock named Izan..."

I won't bore you with the finer professional details of the report, other than to say our veterinarian pathologist, butcher, and baker did an exceedingly dam fine job in identifying the subject's unusual details, contributing factors, what went wrong, and drawing up steps to preclude similar problems from happening again.

In essence, Izan was hungry. His pen gate was open. He went looking for food. He smelled a short distance away some interesting aromas. He went back to his pen and told his muster about it. They all went up in the direction of the smell, namely Mrs Violet White-Walsh's Mudders Restaurant. The side door had been left open. They were attracted to the odour emanating from the Mudders Maundy Thursday Baked Mug Cakes, including, and this is where it gets fascinating, Little Figgy's 60% alcohol-proof brandy aged at least 10 years in oak.

I continue. Izan, the leader of his muster and the most senior bird present, decided he had first rights to all that was in front of him. He gobbled down as many of the Mudders Maundy Thursday Baked Mug Cakes as possible. Too many, it would seem. The alcohol content in them made him dizzy, resulting in him walking around in never-ending circles until his eating habit caused him to choke, resulting in Izan dropping down dead.

Jötunn White, the veterinarian pathologist, butcher on Tuesdays, Thursdays, and Saturdays, baker on Mondays, Wednesdays, and Fridays, and primo uomo singer in the sea shanties and sailing songs category, concluded his report. I quote:

"Death by a loss of control due to a binge eating disorder, by eating unusually large amounts of food over a short period, together with the intake of 60% alcohol-proof brandy, resulting in Izan, Dr Piddy Adfat's prized pet peacock, as

"Death by Misadventure."

Mayor Parsons thanked Jötunn White, Little Figgy's veterinarian pathologist, for his services.

Enosh White-Walsh echoed the mayor's comment with a "Wad-a-Piddy."

On her return to the meeting upon hearing the outcome, Dr Piddy Adfat cried out, "Fowl!"

And as for Yitzhak, as he later remarked quietly to himself in his native language while joining his friend Jötunn White and our Father John Murphy for a beer at Chummy's Pub, "De pave zol nit hobn di sheyne federn, volt zikh keyner a fir nit umgekukt!"*(If the peacock didn't have beautiful feathers, no one would pay any attention to it!).*

"One day, I'll disappear and hide in a corner of Britain. I'll own a bakery in a village, live above it, have a big garden because I like mowing. I want to get up when I feel like it, let people queue for my products, and when they're gone, shut the shop and think about tomorrow. Creating magic - that's my dream. And I'll do it."

-Paul Hollywood

CHAPTER SIX

Burbots Fish and Chips Shop and How One Got Away

Zebedee and Karen Parsons, the owners of Little Figgy's Burbots Fish and Chips Shop, are Pythagorean pescatarians. They will tell you, without a blemish of shame, that they are the only known Pythagorean pescatarians in the village. I will not deny their claim, nor dwell on it.

Zebedee's and Karen's families have the legal rights, dating back hundreds of years, to exclusively fish in the Little Figgy pond for burbot, also called freshwater cod. There are no known other fish in the Figgy pond.

I remember quite clearly a quote I once heard from an inebriated stranger while we both sipped our Moby Pale Ale sitting at the bar at a pub in Anglesea. The pub is called "How One Got

Away". As I'm sure you know, it's located on Wadawurring lands about 20 km from Torquay in Victoria, Australia.

The stranger, I will call him Jack, turned towards me and said, "Mate. All anglers are fishermen, but not all fishermen are anglers."

Jack continued to sip away at his Moby while waiting for a response from me. Little did he know I am not a fisher. But I tried to comfort him with a grunt, a nod of my head, and a shrug. To which he replied, "No worries, Mate. Fair dinkum! No worries!" Jack added, "I'm off to the loo!"

I never saw Jack again.

I repeated my story to Zebedee Parsons while we drank our pint of Little Figgy beer under the canopy of Chummy's pub, facing the Little Figgy pond. He nodded in agreement and repeated Jack's comment with a sigh. "Yes, he's right, you know. All anglers are fishermen, but not all fishermen are anglers." He emphasized the words *not all* quite clearly to me, as if to tell me he was an angler.

Zebedee turned towards me. "Tell me. Do you think Yitzhak the stranger knows how to angle?"

Zebedee's question brought back to me the fascinating conversation I had with Australian Jack and how I replied to him. With a grunt, a nod of my head, and a shrug. It had a similar effect. Zebedee put his beer down on the table, got up, and went to the loo. But unlike Jack, he returned.

It goes without saying that many people who

ask questions are not necessarily looking for an answer, but instead, a compliment. In the case of Zebedee, he already knew from previous questioning that I did not know Yitzhak's angling expertise. I, therefore, recognized there was a suspicious act in the works to which I was not priveé.

"Jesus!" I offered a response to Zebedee. He took the bait.

"Jaysus?" he replied.

"Yes, that's right! Jesus. Well, actually Revelation 7:13-17: 'Then one of the elders answered, saying to me: These who are clothed in the white robes, who are they, and where have they come from?'"

"Ah! I see what you're driving at!" Zebedee retorted with a chuckle. White robes and Yitzhak, eh! I get it!" He didn't!

"You know they bite best at night, after dark," Zebedee added boastfully. There was a pause between night and after dark while he looked at the last remnants of his pint of beer.

"Just over there, facing the Little Figgy pond, that's where they are at night, in deep water." He pointed knowingly with the confidence of a proprietor of a fish and chips shop.

As Olivia, the publican's daughter, passed us, he caught her eye and raised his right index finger in an anti-clockwise circular motion. A few moments later, we had the ownership of another two pints of Little Figgy beer.

"Yes, in deep water, at night. We need a few more anglers, at night, to help us bring in the extra fish."

Zebedee didn't wait for my "why?" before continuing.

"The annual Little Figgy Hootie Music Festival is planned next month, right over there," he pointed at the deepest edge of the Little Figgy pond. "And that's where we plan to have a special place cooking our renowned barbeque burbot dish. Come and join us!"

CHAPTER SEVEN

Our Father John Murphy

John Murphy was welcomed into the church at the young age of 13 years by Father Mathew White-Parsons. John was regarded as a superb chorister as well as being an avid reader. His parents had hopes of him going into managing the village of Little Figgy's forested and woodland areas, just like his dad. But John was devoted to the church's ways. "I have a calling inside me," he would say to his parents.

Over time, he ferociously read many of the philosophy and theology books offered to him by Father Mathew. John Murphy became lost in omphaloskepsis. His friends deserted him as he became more entrenched in church affairs.

"John, there is more to Little Figgy's life than the Gates of Heaven Help Us," his girlfriend at the time, now known as Mayor Sadie Parsons, would say to him. But John was unyielding.

And in time, it came to pass…Father Mathew ordained John Murphy into the priesthood. A few weeks later, Father Mathew voluntarily requested that he be removed from the clerical state for a grave and personal reason, of which we have no further knowledge.

Sadly, he died suddenly on June 29, while our Father John was at his side, on the patio of the Jigs Diner, on the actual day of the 'Little Figgy Fysshynge Wyth an Angle day', after swallowing an entire touton, a hard doughy, fried bread dough ball served with molasses, which he had dipped into his second cup of iced fresh mint tea.

It was left to a shaken, nervous, and youngish our Father John Murphy to conduct the Requiem Mass for his mentor, Father Mathew White-Parsons.

It is said, by those who know our Father John from the old days, that he never recovered from the event, nor did a touton, from that time onward, ever touch his lips.

CHAPTER EIGHT

The Little Figgy Community

O ne early Sunday morning, at Jigs Diner, before the bells of the village church, the Gates of Heaven Help Us, rang out for the annual commemoration service of St. Fiacre, the patron saint for haemorrhoid sufferers.

There they all were, during the twelve days of Christmas, dressed up and wearing face masks to hide their identity, while celebrating the centuries-old Christmas tradition of the Mummers Festival.

They were feasting on either of the two breakfast specials of the day, fish cakes, made with potatoes, burbot, onions, and herbs, served with baked beans, or toutons which are doughy, fried bread dough balls served with molasses or berry jam. As an alternative, the chef's steam-basted fried eggs, lightly sprinkled with cheese.

Both of these decidedly tasty meals are produced

by Chef extraordinaire and owner Luke Brown. I have complimented Chef Brown for his creative ability, handed down from generation to generation.

Luke Brown – a man of respected girth and presence – was hard of hearing. He was also afflicted with Stereotyphobia, a complaint defined as suffering from monotonous repetition, caused by having to repeat too many of his toutons and fried egg orders to his servers.

Jigs Diner, for those of you who aren't conversant with the traditional culinary ancient delights of Newfoundland and Labrador, is named after a hearty comfort meal called Jigs Dinner, which consists of potatoes, cabbage, turnips, carrots, and boiled salt beef. A meal having a unique cultural identity, and I add with utterly no disrespect to its ownership, that today would make an ordinary sophisticated Frenchman and Frenchwoman with any sense of appréciation gastronomique française, want to... well, you get my gist!

But this wasn't France, at least not to the citizens of Little Figgy, who continued after hundreds of years to take their tradition very seriously. It had all to do with custom. Fish cakes, toutons, and Jigs Diner embraced a value they weren't prepared to give up.

Those present that eventful morning, amongst others, included Mayor Sadie Parsons and her husband Jack Parsons, and three of their four children, Jaxon, Jakson, and Jennifer; Chief Constable Gabriel White and his dog Goobies; publican William Brown and his lovely daughter Olivia; our Father John Murphy; Junia, the widow Murphy, who is the church carillonneur and member of the Passalorynchite Christian sect, who years ago, much to the relief and wishes of her neighbours, had taken a vow of perpetual silence; Enosh White-Walsh, the village lawyer; and Dr Piddy Adfat and her husband Baba Younus.

If one wanted to show the utmost respect and benevolence toward the village population, one would say, as I'm doing to you, they were quite an assorted group with medical disorders, including various phobia symptoms. And other than our Father Murphy, Dr Piddy Adfat and her husband Baba Younus, they all could proudly trace their Newfoundlander and Labradorian family roots from one of the Tickle villages, including Tickle Cove, Black Tickle, Chimney Ticklers, Leading Tickles, and Tickle Harbour.

As to the doctor, Piddy Adfat, and Baba Younus, her husband? Out of deference, one never spoke about where they came from, other than to say the doctor was known amusingly by the villagers as Wad-a-Piddy! She had a habit of always shaking her head and raising her shoulders on hearing about an unfortunate event, while whispering to herself, "Wad-a-Piddy!"

Baba Younus to the villagers was commonly known as 'a pain in the ass', which admirably fitted his profession. Baba Younus was a proctologist by profession, but he no longer practiced his occupation, preferring to just be his wife's medical assistant and receptionist. However, he had a calling that was appreciated by the village community.

And then there was our Father John Murphy, who, at this time in his life, had resigned himself to accepting most of his parishioners, other than Junia, the widow Murphy, had given up on religion. He was the only villager who could proudly trace his roots back to a small Newfoundland village called Dildo.

In all honesty, the village cannot by any stretch of the imagination be described as being quintessential. Nor, on the opposite spectrum, could one call it wanting. Quirky or odd might be more appropriate, both in personality and in its population. I do not mean to imply I'm mocking its residents. God forbid! However, even though the village never wanted for anything and was self-sufficient in every manner, it suffered from a population bottleneck, causing, if I can aptly put it to you, a genetic drift that was seeing a decrease in the size of the village's gene pool. This, in itself, led to numerous mental health concerns.

CHAPTER NINE

And How Do You Like Your
Brussels Sprouts?

Not everyone likes Brussels sprouts. I do! Of all the ideas I came up with this past Sunday, one was to visit the Welcome Restaurant in the Welsh village of Little Comely-on-the-Marsh, renowned for its Brussels sprouts.

The restaurant is located on Pricklehill, on the north-east corner of the village, where Brussels sprouts for the villagers is as important as knowing how to prepare a hearty Welsh broth known as cawl.

Upon arrival, I was escorted through a maze of tables and chairs that had experienced another day, and then to a booth that had at one time been described as being cosy and intimate.

Observing the customers, it didn't take very long for the two well-groomed ladies, sitting in a booth close by, to be drawn to my attention.

Their accents were undeniably Welsh.

"I've always liked my Brussels sprouts like my toothbrush, super soft and fluffy."

"My mother-in-law's roasted Brussels sprouts were as hard as a rock."

And with those earth-shaking remarks, a conversation between the two ladies, who obviously were leading gastronomic authorities of their generation, got my interest, as it would yours.

"My David, may he rest in peace, I loved his sprouts. They were always as hard as a rock," remarked Holly. I was introduced to Holly's name by way of the enormous personalized necklace she was wearing. She looked at her friend. "And you, Liliwen. Soft and fluffy?" Liliwen agreed.

Well, for fear of having to contribute to a conversation involving hard and soft and fluffy Brussels sprouts, I immediately called my server over to my table and quietly asked her if there was another booth available for me. There wasn't!

The two ladies, Holly and Liliwen, were beaming at each other, and combined with their combative posture, just six feet away, with Holly scanning me, I was now more than ever certain I had chosen the wrong booth.

Liliwen was the first to order. "I'll have a cup of chicken soup with one small plate of Brussels sprouts, soft and fluffy, with no ginger in it. Ginger's too pungent for me." She turned to Holly. "I'm allergic to ginger, you know. It gives me pain in my stomach! And make sure the soup has enough thinly sliced carrots in it." She again turned to Holly. "For the sweetness."

Holly nodded and patiently waited for her turn to order.

"Ah, yes, my turn!" Holly, who has peripheral vision, gave me a slight glance that I would best describe as wanting my full attention.

"Yes, a large bowl of chicken soup, and I like my Brussels sprouts roasted and hard, not fluffy, so that they're very firm when bitten. And make sure my chicken is organic and the soup is hot'."

A few minutes passed by as the two ladies, in idle chat, waited for their orders.

Now, I am not by character an individual that one might say gets shocked at what I was about to hear from Liliwen, but there are grounds for giving advanced notice. This was one of them.

"Holly, I have something to tell you." What followed wasn't something Holly was expecting from her friend. A friend she had known since her school days.

"I have come out!"

"From where?" replied Holly.

It was obvious Holly was not familiar with the term.

"From spending too long at home trying to decide if I'm…"

Liliwen paused as her cup of chicken soup with her plate of soft and fluffy Brussels sprouts, containing no ginger in it, had arrived. Holly's order followed. And at the rear, my order of chicken soup with the traditional carrots, parsnips, celery, shallots, and sprigs of parsley floating freely on top arrived.

"I have come out!" affirmed Liliwen, looking down at her soup, with tears slowly trickling down her cheeks that settled onto her soup with a plop! A distinctive sobbing sound followed. Each emotive teardrop, upon hitting the surface of her chicken soup, spread over her thinly sliced carrots, which quivered on contact.

I have to admit, the moving scene in front of me was on par with the 2004 film *Eternal Sunshine of the Spotless Mind,* which received a 92% critics' score on the Rotten Tomatoes Tomatometer.

If one wanted to contribute a wish of musical support for Liliwen, for that is what one does under these trying circumstances. I would have requested *Shostakovich - Symphony No. 5 in D minor, Op. 47.* A fitting piece of music that would have brought all the Brussels sprouts' customers to tears. For I readily accepted Liliwen's natural pain of a heroine, having to express herself to her friend, in a public place.

Liliwen raised her head and looked at Holly for support. None came!

"Holly, did you hear what I just said to you? I have come out! O-U-T!" (I put this word in capitals to show you the intense emotion emanating from Liliwen's tearful eyes).

"Yes, I heard you the first time," Holly quietly remarked, looking into Liliwen's eyes.

"Then tell me, what can I do?

With difficulty, I held myself back from offering a

comment. Yes, Holly, tell her, tell her, what *can* she to do?

Holly put down her large soup spoon, moved her plate of hard roasted Brussels sprouts aside, and in the spirit of friendship, picked up one of Liliwen's soft fluffy Brussels sprouts with her right fingers, put the sprout into Liliwen's mouth and said laughingly after reading the dessert menu, "Mmmm, now I've got it! Let's have some Dicky Waffles for dessert!"

"I think of myself... as a troubadour, a village storyteller, the guy in the shadows of the campfire."

-Louis L'Amour

CHAPTER TEN

Personal Gender Pronouns

I will begin with an account of an incident that happened to me a few days ago. It happened while I was eating a yoghurt parfait at my favourite morning diner, commonly known by its patrons as D&F.

I remember it was nine-thirty-ish with all the serving staff at D&F decked out at their stations, united, readily waiting to serve their patrons with their first cup, but not their last, of hot coffee of the day.

It all started during a chat I had with a patron sitting at the next table while he devoured his plate of eggs and onions served with sliced tomato and cucumber and a toasted rye bagel. He offered me his separate portion of creamy coleslaw, which I confirm remained untouched. I declined.

My newfound friend introduced himself as Mathew Power, formerly a Roman Catholic priest and Benedictine monk, originally of Glovers Harbour, population of 55, previously known as Thimble Tickle, located in Newfoundland.

"Formerly?" I questioned.

"Yes, formerly. I am now a laicised priest," he said.

"Oh! That's interesting," I told him. "And I come from a long family line of bodhrán players," I said with the confidence of a professional Celtic drum player. My confidence lasted but a few seconds.

He countered by teasing me. "How ya getting on? Who knit you?"

I responded to his questions with a blank stare.

"So, you're originally from Glovers Harbour? Well, at least you're not from Dildo," I said with the kind of jocularity and knowledge that told him I was familiar with this Newfoundland town.

"Ah, yes," he muttered with a sigh, dismissing my effort at a double entendre as if he had heard it countless times before. He responded with his best efforts. "Do you know we in Glovers Harbour are the giant squid capital of the world? We're still in the *Guinness Book of Records* for the largest squid ever to wash up ashore. 55 feet long it was, along the shore."

"Recently?" I enquired.

"Oh no, in 1878." He paused from eating, leaned over to my table, and whispered, "I'll also tell you something in strict confidence."

"Hold on one minute! I'm not Catholic, I can't hear your confession!" I said with absolute conviction.

"No, no, no! I just want to tell you that some time ago, when I was a locum tenens, I had a bit of an argument with my diocesan bishop and..."

I did not pursue the matter. Prying into the domestic affairs of a former earthly representative of Christ isn't something that infatuates me.

"Really? Well, in that case, how do you now earn your living?" I asked.

"I'm now a dialect and personal gender pronoun coach," he replied.

He looked at me. "And I'm no longer Father Power to my congregation, no, I mean clients." He paused. "I'm called, they!"

They continued while slicing his sliced tomato. "Did you know the use of gender pronouns is not new? Gendered language was documented as early as 1795. And the use of they as a gender-neutral pronoun predates this by some three or four hundred years."

"How on earth do you know this?" I asked.

"Google Research," he replied as he waved at someone walking towards him.

The individual nodded to me as he joined they, the former Father Power.

"This is they." He pointed nonchalantly at his friend. "They recently came out as gender-fluid-non-binary and is also neurodivergent."

"Ah, yes! Oh, how fascinating!" I nodded carefully.

In this story, to distinguish the difference between the two characters, I will now refer to them as they the elder and they the younger.

I moved the conversation to my advantage.

"Just the other day, on Perplexity, did you

know?.." They the elder nodded to me in recognition of my search engine, "I read that the first fax machine was invented by Scottish mechanic and inventor Alexander Bain. In 1843, Alexander Bain received a British patent for "improvements in producing and regulating electric currents and improvements in timepieces and electric printing and signal telegraphs, in laymen's terms a fax machine."

They both turned their heads towards me in awe.

To be quite candid, as I looked around at D&F's other nearby patrons, who were by now deeply engrossed in listening to our conversation, I received a series of nods of encouragement, as if I had established myself on behalf of all gender binaries present.

That is, until I was interrupted by our server. "Would they like she to top up their coffee?"

They the elder responded. "Yes, please. By the way, since my previous visit to D&F, you've changed your non-binary name?"

"Yes," said the server, "she has." And without further ado, she refilled our coffee cups to the brim and walked away.

They the elder looked at me. It was Name the Tickle time. "Did you know the name Tickle is quite common on the island?"

"Is that so?" I responded.

"Yes," they the elder replied. "There's Tickle Cove, Black Tickle, Chimney Tickle, Leading Tickles, and of course Thimble Tickle."

"You can blow me down with all the tickles," I tutted.

"Ah, yes! You're quite a character, aren't you? Then you know of Blow Me Down Provincial Park on the west coast of the island," they the younger responded.

"No, not exactly. I must admit, I'm somewhat witless in knowing the names of all your small communities," I said.

"Well, you little sleeveen! Get out of here! You've been teasing us all along, haven't you? I come from Witless Bay. They must have told you, wha!" said they the younger.

I looked at these two characters facing me, and a quote by Andrew Carnegie came to mind. "As I grow older, I pay less attention to what men say. I just watch what they do."

It's been said that everybody who has reached or passed middle age, as I have, looks back with affection to the time in their youth when everything was quite simple. For my part, I too look back with fondness to the days, a period of time in the past, when it was a joy to just have the choice of ordering a simple breakfast at D&F.

Life today is a complex matter. But as the late Betty White, the comedic actress, said, "It's your outlook on life that counts. If you take yourself lightly and don't take yourself too seriously, pretty soon you can find the humour in our everyday lives. And sometimes it can be a lifesaver."

Today, with all the endless political rambling taking place, we need more lifesavers than politicians to help us return to some normalcy.

And with those thoughts, I finished my yoghurt parfait, called she over, paid the bill, said goodbyes to both theys, and hurriedly left to continue on my errands.

CHAPTER ELEVEN

My Life as a Phytologist

This is an account, as I will now share with you, of my primary reason for visiting the village of Little Comely-on-the-Marsh. It was to seek out Sonchus palmonses and Pastadendron italica.

To those of you who have an absence of Latin in your veins, my reference to Sonchus palmonses and Pastadendron italica does not refer to two famous Roman generals or members of the Senate of the ancient Roman Empire who were murdered.

With the utmost confidence, I express these names to illustrate that I am a part-time phytologist.

For all my adult life, I have had a fascination with botany, not as one of the mill scientists who study plants, but as one who seeks out plants located in isolated communities in the department of Drôme, in southeastern France.

Some of you might throw a little doubt as to my

real purpose, but this is an account based upon my true intentions, where nobody is hurt or dies, nobody gets drunk, and nobody suffers from infrequent bowel movements.

I am simply fascinated by finding the locations of the giant tree dandelion and the spaghetti bush.

On my arrival in Little Comely, I immediately sought after Dr Jacobs, the village's medical doctor, deputy coroner, and pharmacist. At the time, he was on one of his regular Saturday morning walks in the forest, looking for various medicinal plants for the treatment of diseases prevalent in the village population. We struck an instant friendship.

"Ah! Come over here and look at my Ganoderma lingzhi."

Dr Jacobs was, of course, referring to his friend, commonly known as the king of mushrooms. I recognised it immediately as a medicinal mushroom used in Chinese traditional medicine.

"So, you're a Phytologist, are you? Dr Jacobs handed me one of his Ganoderma lingzhi.

"Yes, and also a bit of an amateur ornithologist," I replied, pointing to a tree where a short-toed treecreeper was perched. "Did you know the short-toed treecreeper has shorter toes than the more common treecreeper?"

Dr Jacobs, with his hands full of king mushrooms, acknowledged my authority on the subject and added, "Yes, indeed. And as I'm sure you're aware, it is a known fact that the short-toed nests in tree crevices or bark flakes."

His response established that we had become friends for life, but not, it would seem, in my quest to find the locations of the giant tree dandelion and the spaghetti bush.

"I'm afraid my botanical skills go no further than plant identification for the treatment of diseases of my patients." He paused as he witnessed my jaw dropping towards my hyoid bone. "However, I suggest you meet up with the Fahey-Fizzard twins, Fannie and Hattie. In their youth, they were sheep shearers. They're afternoon regulars at the Welcome Restaurant & Tea Rooms."

I thanked Dr Jacobs for his suggestion and went on my way, muttering under my breath, how could Fannie and Hattie Fahey-Fizzard, the sheep-shearing twins, assist me?

My meeting that afternoon with the sheep-shearing twins, to say the least, had all the makings of a unique theatrical stage event. The story is so fascinating, it is one that I will now share with you.

Fannie and Hattie Fahey-Fizzard appeared slowly from upstage right, walking arm-in-arm, downstage.

Now, at the ripe age of 97 years, they are the last of their dynasty. Throughout their mature lives, they preferred their roles to be those of chameleon thespians. Their deep passion for acting exceeded their preference for sheep-shearing. Neither of them married.

At a young age, their parents obliged them with ancient stories about the indigenous people who traditionally inhabited Newfoundland and Labrador.

Tales of the Beothuk, Innu, and Inuit became bedtime stories. The stories, of which we have no reason to dispute fascinated the girls, and over the years, every Sunday afternoon at the Little Comely Cultural Centre, to a packed house, they would perform as heroines of a bygone age.

But now, suffering from acute spectrophobia, they reluctantly decided to retire from the theatre world, preferring these days to take their place every Monday and Friday at the Welcome Restaurant & Tea Rooms, sipping on their green tea amongst regular patrons, quietly acknowledging with a smile and a twinkle in their eyes anyone who recognised them. Very few did!

Fannie and Hattie stepped forward and approached me. Hattie, in her left hand, carried a priceless zamphona, a medieval six-string instrument, while her right hand offered me an off-white facial tissue. Fannie, in the meantime, greeted me with four emotional words a playwright would die for! "Hattie, hide the silver!"

As it's been said before, no theatre director could have accomplished such a visual or emotional effect as what was witnessed by all those watching the event.

Fannie and Hattie, or for the sake of simplicity, I will now call them the Fahey-Fizzard twins, originally grew up in the village of Little Figgy, but when their parents separated they moved for some years to the village of Little Pletzl where they listened to stories of how, in the old country, their father's family were involved in raising sheep.

The stories fascinated the girls, and as they grew up, they vowed to become sheep shearers. Their story now becomes more than interesting.

As it's been written by their biographer, one early spring sunny afternoon, while on their walk among Little Pletzl's bushes and shrubs, they came across a small flock of lost Préalpes-du-Sud sheep wandering aimlessly in front of them. Without any consequences of the laws governing the stealing of sheep, they somehow stole the sheep and...

Thereafter, the girls fled and somehow, I know not how, ended up here in Little Comely.

I have to admit, even though I have Welsh Wales blood in me, I know nothing about sheep, nor can I distinguish the difference between a Little Pletzl Préalpes-du-Sud from an Arles Merinos breed.

What I can say to you now, with utter conviction, I am sure the Fahey-Fizzard twins, if they had stayed in Little Pletzl, would have had a good chance of becoming Golden Shears World Sheep Shearing and Wool Handling Champions. I can accept that was their commitment to raising sheep. But all this happened so long ago.

My afternoon with the Fahey-Fizzard twins flew by faster than finding a snow flea on one's belly button.

At the end of the day, I invited them back to my temporary living quarters where I made us all homemade roasted eggplant and pickled beet sandwiches, accompanied by some of Dr Jacob's Ganoderma lingzhi. And while we shared nostalgic memories of long-gone times, my original quest of seeking out the locations of the giant tree dandelion and the spaghetti bush was all but forgotten.

"I am a simple man who comes from a village, and villagers like us speak our mind. Now, in the process, if unknowingly my words came across as disrespectful or insulting, then I am deeply sorry. I don't want to hurt anyone."

-Arijit Singh

CHAPTER TWELVE

The Baked Apple and H-cups.

Tradition dictates I tell you a story that happened at La Pomme au Four, a small, charming country café located in the vicinity of our three villages. The café owes its fame to its, yes, baked apples, and their creator Philis de la Charce of the Château de la Charce, the heroine of Dauphiné. She died on June 4, 1703.

You may wonder at this time what connection this has to do with the content of my anthology. It doesn't! But it is a fascinating story.

Every June 4 at four in the afternoon, three ladies headed to La Pomme au Four for coffee and the sharing of three baked apples. They always sat together at their regular spot located at the rear of the café under a portrait of Philis de la Charce.

The ladies loved to talk incessantly. Clarisse was the shyest of the three. Impeccably dressed, she wore

Italian designer-style boots, a pair of large prescription dark glasses, a grey cashmere and a silk jacket, accompanied by a long black skirt.

Celina in her youth had been the quietest of the trio. At one time, she had been her community's quintessential certified marieuse, a matchmaker. Her infinite wisdom was regarded with the utmost respect by the younger members of her community and their parents alike. Her record of success was second to none. She abounded with enthusiasm and energy that would put Eliezer, the servant of Abraham, the matchmaker for Abraham's son Isaac, relegated to the second choice.

Regrettably, the combination of religion and politics was not a subject treated with respect by Celina. As the exclusive certified community matchmaker, it was her sworn duty to uphold the primary tenet of her trade. Thou must not be a busybody.

As she grew older, she became a blabbermouth. Her unrestrained views on how the community was run exceeded the bounds of good breeding. She started to wear a red shawl with the letters MOCGA boldly inscribed around her shoulders. "Make Our Community Great Again" became her mantra. Celina was decertified as a marieuse soon after.

Chloé completed the group of three. Widowed at a young age she had been a supreme advocate of the roll-your-own cigarette and gambling fraternity. There was never a time without a cigarette dangling out of her mouth, supplemented by the ash on her enormous natural H-cup breasts, which, with a brush of her right hand, eventually found its way down to her tiny waist.

She was proud of her tiny waist was Chloé. So much so that at all of her social events over time, it became a tradition to tell the story about her tiny waist and her baked apple.

One Sunday afternoon at La Pomme au Four, Chloé sat at a table with her family. It wasn't a particularly dysfunctional family, other than to say they incessantly argued with each other. They each ordered baked apples.

Well, to continue. While eating, Chloé keeled over and she ended up with her H-cups temporarily assigned to sitting gracefully on her nephew Claude's half-eaten baked apple.

Thankfully, Chloé's two nieces, Sherrica and Sherenna, managed to guide her to the nearest female-friendly washroom, where they cleaned her up and diagnosed the problem. Chloé's under-bust corset was too tight.

The two nieces, guided by the principles of decency, said nothing on their return. On the other hand, they removed all the remaining portions of baked apple and, with a flourish, deposited Chloé's corset on the table for all to see.

Chloé, in front of all La Pomme au Four patrons and staff, standing on her chair, flouting her H-cups, responded magnificently in her best alpine Provençal dialect. "Un monde où les gens ne se soucient pas de La Pomme au Four, c'est comme comparer mes gros seins à des raisins secs!" *(A world where people don't care about baked apples is like comparing my big breasts to raisins!).*

From that day onwards, La Pomme au Four never again served baked apples on Sunday, even though, for tradition, it remained on their menu.

CHAPTER THIRTEEN

Yitzhak, the Stranger

Don't you agree, that there's always at least one character in a crowd who immediately stands out as someone worth noting? I speak here from experience in choosing, as my first candidate, Yitzhak, a man of extraordinary demeanour and personality, and one who is markedly oddball. He is a student of philology and knowledgeable in the field of linguistics in languages such as Frantsoydish, English, Yiddish, Hebrew, Punjabi, French, Welsh, and Mesopotamian Arabic.

But, I wonder, is that odd? Well, I shall do my best for you, for the sake of clarity, to tell you a little more about my friend Yitzhak, formally known as Captain Idris, since he plays a central part in my anthology.

Yitzhak lived in the villages of Little Comely-on-the-Marsh, an eccentric Welsh community with 347 inhabitants, Little Pletzl-on-the-Zump, a community of some 613 Yiddish-speaking residents, and recently, he found his way to Little Figgy-on-the-Duff. All three of these villages, as you now are aware, are located in the department of Drôme in southeastern France. I admit, I have had cause to visit them all.

The villages were something from another era, living up to the expectations, traditions, and rituals that no longer existed in their citizens' home countries. The villages were self-sufficient in every aspect, never needing to introduce anything French into their villages. No French veggies, fruit, or meat for them, and indeed no French wine, and certainly I will emphasize no potatoes! The villagers know who precisely they are, and strange as it might seem, it remains a mystery that all three villages, even though they are but a short distance from each other, do not know of each other's existence.

Yitzhak was known in Little Comely as Captain Idris, the village's 89-year-old legal representative. He knew everything there was to know about 12th-century Welsh law called *Cyfraith Hywel*, but little else. Captain Idris, self-appointed in the uniform of a WWI Royal Flying Corps pilot, decked himself out with a leather hat and goggles, the traditional white silk scarf, and a leather jacket. He had a companion named Aelwen, a life-size blow-up doll, dressed to kill and always attached to the Captain's left foot.

Two years later, in the village of Little Pletzl, Captain Idris appeared and identified himself as Yitzhak.

Yitzhak was an unusual character, even by Little

Pletzl's standards. He was at the time a hard-of-hearing 91-ish year-old court jester figure, who had become one of the best Jewish law and jurisprudence minds in his village of 613 Jewish souls. He knew everything there was to know about Halakha, the laws derived from the written and Oral Torah.

In a short time, he gained a constant companion by the name of Shprintza, who in her youth was regarded as an accomplished four-key bassoonist. This bassoon is looked upon as the most difficult woodwind instrument to master since it demands all ten fingers to play.

Unfortunately, one evening while cutting up some hard cheese for Yitzhak, the knife slipped and she lost her left index finger to a very sharp knife. I ask you to give some serious thought to the situation, for it affected their relationship, which, at the time, was also going through some difficulty. You see, how should I put it? Well, I wouldn't say Shprintza was an alcoholic, but she had the reputation of finishing a large glass of the region's finest wine before you could say "Blessed is the Creator of the fruit of the vine."

After Yitzhak's relationship with Shprintza ended, he became agitated and reckless, causing him to have fits of depression and memory loss, all of which led him to decide on a career change.

At the age of 94 years, he entered a period of self-isolation, resulting in him becoming a self-proclaimed orthodox Jewish guru, the traditional kind, wearing white clothing, comprising upper and lower garments with open Jesus sandals. On top of his man bun grey hair, a white yarmulke adorned his head.

Based on his mission, he took a suitable name, Gurdayal the Compassionate, as a means of becoming the first spiritual vegan advisor and leader to the youth of Little Pletzl. His ultimate vision was to create a new vegan-based life for himself and the youth.

His idea was of course utterly noble, and he gained a great following until he was found one Saturday morning to be eating honey. He was a mellivore! He enjoyed eating honey! Startled, his vegan youth minions rebelled and called him a fraud.

With his secret now discovered and with a lack of support from his village friends, completely dispirited, he felt he had no option but to leave Little Pletzl and travel into the unknown for the second time in his life.

As he left Little Pletzl, walking slowly towards the forest, he stopped, turned, and looked back at all the curiosity seekers who had come to watch his parting. He gestured to them in a manner not unlike in the olden days, when groups of wives waved goodbye to their Newfoundland fishermen husbands leaving for the Grand Banks. And with a flask of honey in his right hand, he smiled and addressed them all:

"Effective immediately I, Yitzhak with one of best Jewish law and jurisprudence minds in Little Pletzl, who knows everything there is to know about Halakha, the laws derived from the written and Oral Torah, who entered a period of becoming an orthodox Jewish guru with the name of Gurdayal, the Compassionate the self-proclaimed spiritual vegan advisor and mentor to the youth of Little Pletzl, effective immediately abandons all that surrounds me.

"I intend to follow the travels of Gershon ben Eliezer ha-Levi and write an account of my journey, crossing the impossible Sambation River, beyond which, as it has been told, the Ten Lost Tribes of Israel were banished by the Assyrian king Shalmaneser V."

And with those rather touching, overemotional and historical words, he disappeared into the forest.

Two years later, now at the age of 96 years, while walking amongst the bushes and twigs, he came across an oak tree where a short-toed treecreeper was perched. He gestured at the bird and said laughingly in his native language, "Nu! Az me ken nit me vil, muz men vellen vi me ken!" (*Come* on*! If you can't do what you like, you must like what you can do!*). Thereafter, as he turned to continue on his journey, he tripped and, in falling, his flask of honey hit him above his right eye with such force that our voyager passed out.

Days later, at the Jigs Diner in the village of Little Figgy-on-the-Duff, as patrons were feasting on their breakfast, the Diner's door opened and in an episode taken right out of an epic religious drama located in Roman-occupied Judea, Yitzhak came out of the shadows with blood streaming down his face above his right eye, and his hands profusely bleeding. He was also short of one of his open Jesus sandals.

I pause so that you can compose yourself before I continue.

It was our Father John Murphy, who observing this dramatic scene, stood up and with fear in his eyes, crossed himself and initiated the first contact with Yitzhak.

"Lord tundering Jaysus!"... thereafter, as his voice trailed off, Yitzhak fell with his bleeding face landing between our Father John Murphy's plate of two poached eggs.

My friends, I would be utterly surprised if you didn't question me as to how I knew about all these happenings. I will therefore respond in this way. Simply put, to quote Nicolaus Copernicus, "To know that we know what we know, and to know that we do not know what we do not know, that is true knowledge."

CHAPTER FOURTEEN

The Annual Mari Lwyds Festival of Concert, Song, Poetry, and Prayer, and Penelope, the graffiti artist

The average reader, I have no doubt, will not know of the Mari Lwyds Festival that takes place on March 1st, St David's Day. It is the highlight of the year for the vast majority of Little Comely's village population. It is a day of splendid Welsh choir music, mixed with the finest poetry and dance, some dating back hundreds of years. But, there was something exclusive that set the festival in a different category from all other celebrations.

The Mari Lwyd, in itself, comprises an artificial horse skull, adorned with stunning decorations, such as coloured ribbons, all fastened to a long pole. Attached to the back of the skull is a white sheet draped down to hide the individual holding up the pole.

Some might call it a legendary love story dating back to the laws set down by the ancient druids in the 10th century AD, but with a twist. Instead, as tradition dictated of a white-robed druid climbing an oak tree to cut down mistletoe with a golden sickle, Little Comely's early historians gave a different account. You see mistletoe was banned by the elders. So in its place, holly was used as an integral part of the village's annual festival. And this is where Penelope, one of the village's registered nurses, appears in my story.

Penelope, a registered nurse, and a dam fine good one, had in her mind always wanted to become one of the foremost artists of the European street graffiti period. She had eased into it several years ago when caught in the act of drawing a graffiti piece of Mildred Hastings, the Mayor's wife, sitting on a gold toilet seat.

If that wasn't enough to create an impression, she attached it to the exterior wall of The Duke of Wellington pub, facing the village pond.

Her work created quite an interest. Many villagers tried to see the symbolism in the artwork. School children, restricted only to those in the most senior grade, were assigned to write a project about it. Mayor Hastings, who was also the Justice of the Peace, eventually decided he had better charge Penelope with some offence, even though he acknowledged the graffiti, at a specific angle, did resemble his wife. In due course, Penelope was charged and put on probation for one year.

Just by chance, the artistic director of Little

Comely's Community Arts & Crafts Centre had seen Penelope's creative skills and suggested to the Justice of the Peace that she take Penelope under her wing and guide her to a more respected medium of the traditional Welsh art world. Penelope propelled herself into it and eventually produced hundreds of *Mari Lwyds*. They were all used during Little Comely's Annual International Mari Lwyds Festival of Concert, Song, Poetry and Prayer.

The Festival started at nine in the morning. If Wellesley Llewellyn, the publican of the Duke of Wellington, had been allowed to open his pub at that hour, he would have done some grand business. However, all the villagers came down to the village pond, surrounded it with their individual *Mari Lwyds,* and deposited the poles with the horses' skulls into the water, which were then pushed out to the centre of the pond. There, one of Little Comely's single young ladies, decked out in her traditional Welsh costume, *Gwisg Gymreig draddodiadol*, would stand up in a Welsh boat waiting to receive the first Mari Lwyd of the season. Picking it out of the water and holding it high above her head gave her the right to choose a suitable lover.

Last year, with great enthusiasm, Penelope was chosen for this honoured task. Regrettably, not one Mari Lwyd reached her. They all sank, and in a fit of irrational behaviour, she lost her balance, tipped the boat, and fell into the water.

I have comfort in knowing she survived. It was after this incident that Penelope decided to focus more on her graffiti artistic ability.

The Village School, or as the locals knew it, "Ysgol y Pentref", backed onto the home of Mrs Nala Angharad-Snomis, the school's head teacher. Everyone in the community respected her. Every person simply called her Mrs Angharad, for her name, as you may be aware, dates back to the twelfth century.

Angharad was the wife of Gruffudd ap Cynan, king of Gwynedd. He became revered as King of all Wales and was a significant figure in Welsh resistance to Norman rule. This story in itself, relating to the demise of anything purporting to be French, was enough to put Mrs Angharad on a pedestal.

However, Mrs Angharad, now on maternity leave, was well past her due date, and Dr Jacobs was becoming somewhat concerned. Inducing labour might be the best option.

It was Penelope who resolved the problem. As per her agreement with Mrs Angharad, she created one of her artistic graffiti masterpieces in celebration of the future birth. Her work surrounded the outside door frame of Mrs Angharad's front door.

The result was extraordinary visual in concept. So much so that the first and only time Mrs Angharad saw it, her water broke, and she immediately went into labour. Penelope called her work "The Delivery of the Placenta." It was the last commission she received before returning to full-time nursing.

CHAPTER FIFTEEN

Walkless dogs I have met in my time

If I may, I will tell you I have recently noted the abundance of little dogs, all shapes, colours, and sizes, residing in the village of Little Pletzl. Let me say, in all honesty, I adore the canine animal. Call it what you wish, pooch, doggy, pet, or simply der Hund!

I mention these details because, astonishingly as it may seem, Pletzl's little dogs do not walk. My first reaction was to presume they suffered from degenerative myelopathy or hind leg paralysis. I was wrong!

No! They are simply held under their owner's left armpit and by the look of the expression in their eyes, the pooches are quite comfortable in this position.

The term "walkies" has a very different meaning in Pletzl.

Take for instance, Malvina and Kini, two ladies also known by their stage names, Malvineeta and

Kinieeta, the names I will now address them.

Every day, except Saturday, at ten in the morning, the ladies can be seen together, with their little pooches held tightly under their left armpits, heading towards Zee Bee Dairy Bakery where they sit outside on the patio, drink a glass of green tea, and eat one shared slice of pecan butter tart.

Like many thespians who incessantly love to sing, Malvineeta and Kinieeta act in character on and off the stage. Take last Sunday. Malvineeta, the smaller of the two, wore huge platform shoes to compensate for her lack of height. In addition, together with a pair of large dark sunglasses, a bright yellow jacket, and skin-tight black leggings, she looked the epitome of someone who had just participated in *Monty Python's Lumberjack Song*.

There is no use in pretending about it, Kinieeta was the quieter of the two. She didn't have much of a choice. For most of her conversation with Malvineeta, she was relegated to simply nodding her head. There is no doubt she was the understudy of this twosome.

As to the two pooches, I never once heard their owners calling them by name. They sat there communicating in a silent language to each other, eye-to-eye, snout-to-snout, while their owners, with their left fingers, tickled them under their ears and in coordination ate a shared slice of pecan butter tart with their right fingers.

CHAPTER SIXTEEN

I am a Turophile

I am a turophile, I can assure you, not just an insignificant turophile, as I have been called many times in my life, but a noteworthy turophile. Simply put, I am a lover of cheese, a young soft cheese before it matures, that is.

The cheese in question is named Chèvre nue, which is made with goat's milk containing an occasional spicy taste, with understated flavours of mushrooms and hazelnuts. It is, of course, as I'm sure you are aware, paired with fresh sweet fruits and crusty bread.

I indulge myself in just thinking of it.

Two eating establishments come immediately to mind that exceed my expectations of delivering to me on a plate my favourite soft cheese. You may also know of them. Both have attained Michelin accreditation and are located southwest of Route D61 and the forests of Commune d'Establet and the Ruisseau d'Establet in the department of Drôme.

The Potchke Restaurant and Russian Tea Rooms is where Chef Glucke recently took over the restaurant after the unexpected death of her husband, famed Michelin Chef Nahum, of blessed memory, a man of great girth and a mouth of comparable size. He died one early morning while sucking on a cooked chicken's left paw that had become lodged in his throat.

The Welcome Restaurant and Tea Rooms is under the direction of renowned chef and countertenor opera singer Meurig ap Griffiths. He has a lineage dating back to the early Welsh kings. Regardless of the restaurant's Michelin status, this in itself secured his right, by his customers, to produce his exceptional cuisine, as well as listening to him sing, with great gusto, the title role in Handel's Julius Caesar as he made himself a Welsh rarebit and a nice cup of tea.

However, writing about my beloved soft cheese gets harder and harder for me, especially when I start comparing the health benefits of my Chévre nue served at the restaurants owned by the celebrated names of Chef Glucke and Chef Meurig ap Griffiths. In essence, at my senior age, it all boils down to my tooth enamel and crusty bread, a combination that must both work in harmony to produce a satisfying conclusion the next time I visit my dentist.

CHAPTER SEVENTEEN

Blodwin's Family Day

On February 17, we celebrate Family Day. It offers, as they say, an opportunity for families to reconnect and support their bonds through mutual experiences and quality time spent together.

And what better way is there to experience the day than by telling you a story that I dedicate to Blodwin.

My story is called "Blodwin's Family Day". The pub, The Duke of Wellington, is the village of Comely's centre of social activity. It forms an essential part of the village. Sadly, after the unfortunate drowning of Blodwin, the publican's daughter, the pub for a while became a more subdued establishment. It lost some of its energy. Also, the beer for Hairy Hu Gardan, of council village fame, he was never an elected official, didn't taste the same.

Blodwin, the publican's buxom daughter, on one of her daily afternoon walks, had spotted two male friends sprawled out on the other side of the village pond, eating fish and chips. From the opposite side of the pond, she waved at them, hopeful by chance, they would recognise her. She was not disappointed.

With that encouraging sign, she walked towards them with the stride of a determined publican's daughter as she hastily checked her appearance, making sure her mascara wasn't running and her hair was perfect,

Her Duke of Wellington red, white and green baseball cap with the words "Y Ddraig Goch" *(the red dragon)* written on the crown was firmly on her head, and Kynan, her dad's Welsh corgi, was close by her side.

One could say her approach wasn't particularly novel for someone of her young age; other than that, Blodwin had a unique side to her personality. She was known to have a fetish for malt vinegar. At an astonishing distance of 25 metres, Blodwin's ears would start flapping, her nose would start sniffing, and her eyes would focus on her objective. Lord help us if anyone was in her way!

It was on this glorious afternoon, with the sun shining directly on her face and her respiratory allergies acting up, that her stride toward her destination took on an entirely new energy. All thoughts about her dad, Wellesley Llewellyn, coping by himself back at the pub, were obliterated from her mind. For now, she whiffed the malt vinegar lying on top of the crunchy chips, accompanied with a spoonful of tartar sauce for the fish, sent young Blodwin in a tizzy! Regrettably, within fifteen metres of reaching her objective, she slipped on some Canada Geese poop, fell into the water, hit her head on a stone, and drowned.

It was Monday morning at ten o'clock at The Coroner's Office. They were all there for the inquest, dressed in black, to pay their respects. Devastated, they were. The Coroner opened the investigation without a post-mortem examination. However, he did gain evidence from Blodwin's two male friends.

They stated, under oath, that they were having such a grand time together eating their fish and chips, that they didn't hear Blodwin approaching them. Now, in the real world beyond the village, one would not hesitate to suggest, with some justification, how this could have happened. When asked that question by the Coroner, the two friends stated they only realised there was a problem when they noticed Kynan, the corgi, running around in circles with Blodwin's baseball cap in his mouth. By that time, Blodwin, who couldn't swim, had wretchedly sunk to the 3.6 metres depth of the village pond.

With that information, the Coroner issued the Medical Certificate of Cause of Death as "By accidental death by drowning."

In the time-honoured village tradition, before the funeral, the wake lasted for several nights. Wellesley Llewellyn, Blodwin's dad, insisted the wake had to be held at his pub. For not only was that where his daughter had worked, but also in consideration of his agoraphobia. Everyone agreed. It was the right thing to do since free beer and sandwiches were planned.

Blodwin's funeral was an affair to remember. Penelope, the graffiti artist and nurse, was commissioned by the village council to create a vibrant graffiti depicting Blodwin's life, a task that even Salvador Dali would have had difficulty accomplishing. And with the utmost enthusiasm, Penelope produced a life-size image of Blodwin with her red baseball cap on her head and dressed as a bottle of her favourite malt vinegar, floating in the pond. Magically painted above her head were the Latin words "Blodwin. Nos memores sumus vestri. Edere in caelis" *(Blodwin. We remember you. Eat in heaven).*

All the villagers came to pay their respects to Penelope's work, which she had painted over the front door of Owen Jones' Fish and Chips shop. It was, as Blodwin's father said at the time, gazing at Penelope's masterful work of his daughter, "Yes, my Blodwin, I think she would have liked it!"

From that day onwards, the day became known as "Blodwin's Family Day", to be celebrated annually on February 17, Family Day. The villagers would come down to Owen Jones' Fish and Chips shop to pay their reverences to one of their own. And to Owen Jones's credit, he offered all the youngsters a free half-portion of chips sprinkled with, as he called it, "Blodwin's Famous Malt Vinegar."

CHAPTER EIGHTEEN

The Trill of the Short-Toed Treecreeper

You, the reader, might very well ask me the question, where in the heart of the department of Drôme in southeastern France will one find the oldest surviving village market, surrounded by forested hills and ridges, striking gorges, olive trees, and eye-catching lavender fields? And, without the slightest hesitation, I will answer you, you won't!

By that, I do not mean to imply the region doesn't have some fascinating medieval buildings and abbatial churches, such as The Gates of Heaven Help Us. And, as it has been said, the region oozes with nature and isolation, where one can hear the trill of the short-toed treecreeper. "Tweetutwee-too-tittit...tweetutwee-too-tittit." But the oldest surviving village market in southeastern France? Nah!

However, I do have an interesting account to

share with you about one village in the region, Little Pletzl, where, hundreds of years ago, the village elders decreed that tradition and community ball games were an integral part of their village way of life.

It was said that the game of Pökelpiłka was originally created by Eastern European-speaking seniors hundreds of years ago in the old country. They had become bored and lethargic with their solitary, unfulfilled lifestyle. All their children and grandchildren had moved away from the family home. No one connected with them or visited them anymore. Social isolation set in, and all that was left were groups of Omas and Opas who sat facing each other at the local eating house, nibbling on their favourite snack, the kosher dill pickle.

What was needed, as the grandparents discussed their situation, was something to keep them socially and cognitively engaged.

"Besides eating kosher dill pickles, we need to create a game to challenge our physical and mental condition," remarked one Opa. "Perhaps a ball game?" he added.

Over several months and with much trial, error, and argument, the seniors developed a ball game that, in essence, helped to improve their sense of purpose.

One creative Oma came up with a suitable name for the game. "Pökel" derived from the

German word meaning salt and brine, and "Piłka", from the Polish word meaning ball.

Little Pletzl's Pökelpiłka, in time became known by its English name "Pickleball", spread throughout the Eastern European communities, and as the population spread westward, leagues and associations were formed in many cities.

Years later, one such league, exclusively for seniors, was established in Little Pletzl, where Pökelpiłka became the national sport of the village. Teams were formed through the auspices of the Little Pletzl Pökelpiłka Players Association, and four indoor courts under one roof were built, accompanied by a surrounding landscape.

Originally, a site just north of where the Little Pletzl Pökelpiłka Players Association now play Pökelpiłka was selected. Unfortunately, at that time, in their enthusiasm, the elders didn't take into account that the area was not only saturated with a marsh, but it was also a breeding area for Muscovy Ducks and Canada Geese.

So, an alternative site was agreed upon, located on the south side of the Little Pletzl pond, between where Zelda and Motti Medical Centre and Zemel's Bakery are today.

And for the first time in history, the courts were designated and named as having first-gender pronouns. She/her/hers and he/him/his, as well as they, became the norm.

"Where I grew up, in a remote village at the back of a valley, the old still thought the dead needed attending to - a notion so universal, it's inscribed in all religions. If you didn't, they might exact revenge upon the living."

-W. G. Sebald

CHAPTER NINETEEN

The Fysshynge Wyth an Angle day and the European Longhorn Beetle
To be explained later in this story

Margaret Brown, the Executive Director of the Little Figgy Cultural Centre, is an outstanding vexillographer. Handed down from generation to generation, today, there isn't anyone in the village who knows more about how to design a bunting flag than our Margaret. For generations, her family has been regarded as the village vexillologists.

I have to admit, if at all possible, I might want to give serious consideration to nominating Margaret Brown to be the next president of The International Fabric Bunting Federation of the Vexillological Association.

Our Margaret, after serious reflection, put together a worthy eclectic, and dynamic group of Little Figgy

Flag Committee members including, Rosie White-Walsh the daughter of Violet White-Walsh of Mudders Restaurant, Wayne Brown-White, the village's Entomologist, sports psychohistorian, Tanith Immilla Walsh, Olivia Brown the daughter of William Brown the publican of Chummy's Pub, and Jötunn White the baker, butcher, and veterinary pathologist.

On hand during the first afternoon of the Little Figgy Flag Committee members' meeting, our Father John Murphy, ever-present at all these propitious occasions, was asked to say a prayer.

"For all those present today, I ask you to bless this meeting. Provide us with your support…" He paused, took a deep breath, and raised his teary right eye upward. "Prepare us all for those we will encounter afterwards. Ready us to make every moment count. Amen."

Amen indeed! Ah yes! The circumstances of what I know of our Father John Murphy's teary-eyed condition would lead us to believe he might be going through some difficult personal issues relating to his religious convictions. This leads me to tell you of what little I know, or for that matter, what anyone knows about the inner workings during that eventful day, of our Father John Murphy.

The morning had started rather cloudy, but by mid-morning, the sun was in full flair. The Little Figgy Pond was surrounded by a profusion of multi-coloured bunting flags with tiny burbots on them in celebration of the event. Each fabric flag had been carefully made at the Little Figgy Community Centre under the patronage of the Little Figgy Flag Committee in support and coordination efforts to enhance good neighbourly relations during appropriate holidays and events.

I honestly believe if there is one day in the year that is celebrated more than any other in Little Figgy, it is without doubt the festival of the 'Little Figgy Fysshynge Wyth an Angle day', fêted since 1495, every year on June 29. To us simple ordinary folk, you might know it as International Fisherman's Day.

It was earlier this year that Mayor Sadie Parsons, without any prior notice, announced the appointment of Zebedee and his wife Karen Parsons of Burbots Fish and Chips Shop as her choice to be Little Figgy's joint honorary chairs of the event.

"I believe we have found and appointed exactly who we need to lead our 'Fysshynge Wyth an Angle day'," she proudly announced as loudly as possible while eating her fish cakes, made with potatoes, burbot, onions, and herbs, served with baked beans, and a side order of boiled eggs, to all those who would listen to her at the regular Sunday morning breakfast at Jigs Diner.

I can say to you upon reflection that the Mayor's decision was not unexpected, but it did cause other questions to be entertained by some members of her cabinet at their Monday lunch at Mudders Restaurant before Little Figgy's council meeting.

Present were Mayor Sadie Parsons, Deputy Mayor Lisa Walsh, the Executive Committee members led by our Father John Murphy, Zebedee Parsons, Enosh Walsh-White, Business Manager Annie White-Brown, and Dr Piddy Adfat.

Enosh Walsh-White, as he always attempted to do, initiated the conversation.

"Yes, I saw it all this morning, at the Jigs Diner, on the patio, in front of everyone. All three of them, hugging and crying, talking in some sort of foreign language while they sipped on their second cup of coffee, with their lures, nets, and tackle boxes strewn all over the place!"

"Wad-a-Piddy," responded Dr Piddy Adfat. "Baba, my husband, has some serious reservations about, you know, the three strangers."

"Yes, I know what you mean, but some of my customers think, in friendship, Karen and I should ask them to be on our Fysshynge wyth an Angle day committee," piped in Zebedee Parsons. "They admit they know very little about Figgy angling, let alone what a burbot is. And as far as the Little Figgy pond, they spend hours at the edge reflectively thinking about something or other."

"Perhaps they thinks they can walk on water," added Annie White-Brown, with a quiet smirk on her face as she glanced at our Father John Murphy.

"Tundering Jaysus! Enough!" screamed our Father John Murphy as he stood up, bright red with rage, banging his fist down on the table. "Have you all lost your minds? O mi Iesu, dimitte nobis debita nostra, salva nos ab igne inferni, perduc in caelum omnes animas, praesertim eas, quae misericordiae tuae maxime indigent."

And with those words, reflecting his views on hate and mercy, he stormed out of Mudders Restaurant as the lunch erupted into chaos.

Our Father John Murphy took the long way back to his beloved church, The Gates of Heaven Help Us. He strolled past the Little Figgy Medical Centre with its muster of peacocks and peahens pecking at the ground, and he passed the Tea & Teeth Co-op Grocery Store. Thereafter, after stopping for a quick pint of Little Figgy beer at Chummy's pub, he stopped at Gabriel White's constabulary to pat Goobies, the police dog. From there he went past the Figgy Diner, not stopping to acknowledge the many whaddya ats. Finally, when arriving at his church he paused and looked up above the church's entrance at the old plaque with the words, "Quaerite primum regnum dei", (*See ye first the kingdom of God*), and referring to the village's strangers, with a tear in his right eye he mumbled to himself, "Whoever you are, this is our event. The Festival is ours! It is time for you to disappear, or return home to your family."

The Festival has a long tradition. It was inspired by the original elders of the village to value nature and to exclusively preserve and celebrate the villagers' unique community spirit. Since 1495, no stranger had participated in the event.

The current year's event was undoubtedly set to be the largest one-day festival to be held in Little Figgy. The event included traditional sea shanties and sailing songs performed by the seniors of the village, and for the first time, a custom-made wooden stage for both performers and anglers located at the very deep edge of the pond facing Chummy's Pub was approved by the Little Figgy Council's Cabinet.

Designed by the husband and wife team, Benjamin and Berthina Brown, professionally known throughout the village as 'The Coopers'. By trade, they made wooden barrels.

As pointed out to me by publican William Brown, "There's no one else in the village that knows more about bulge hoops, cants, or bottom heads than our Ben and Berthina." He added with a smile, "Take Berthina, she knows exactly how to head a barrel." He paused, trying to be kind. "But do either of them know how to design and put together a stage? I don't think so!"

I underlined the words to set the scene for a theatrical mishap that occurred during the opening number performed by Little Figgy's Silver Songsters' Senior Choir. The stage trap door collapsed, accompanied by parts of the stage floor and the buntings. And if that wasn't enough, all the seniors slid one by one into the deepest part of the Little Figgy pond, while they were boisterously singing an a cappella rendering of the last two lines of the first chorus of *Tickle Cove Pond*, accompanied by primo uomo Jötunn White.

Thankfully, every one of the members of the choir could swim as they, dripping wet, upon getting out of the water, and bravely still singing without missing a single musical note, hastily fled into Chummy's Pub for a pint.

But wait! Also prepare yourself for some depressing news. Unfortunately all three strangers who were fishing at the far edge of the stage couldn't swim.

And there's more! It was not as fruitful for the European Longhorn beetle, or as you might know it as the hylotrupes bajulus, the primary initiator of the mishap. The species are not particularly known to be good swimmers, nor can they sing a single a cappella note. However, they are exceptionally good at eating wood.

"I was born in a mining village, and you either played football or played football. If you didn't play, there was something wrong with you."

-Alan Hansen

CHAPTER TWENTY

You are all my Brothers and Sisters

Very few Little Pletzl villagers realise how satisfying it is for me to have a traditional dairy lunch at Zemel's Bakery. My lunch consists of cabbage soup, stuffed peppers, hard-boiled eggs, potato latkes, cheese blintzes, and spinach salad. Pletzl bread sprinkled with cooked onions and poppy seeds, and hot black tea adds to the order.

During my final days in Little Pletzl, after giving it some thoughtful consideration, I invited four of Little Pletzl's personalities to join me for lunch.

The first to arrive was Abe. Abe has a minority ownership in Little Pletzl's broiler and layer chicken farm. He's an unappealing, poorly-dressed, short, bald, pot-bellied, rotund, lisp-speaking, short-sighted womaniser, who's utterly concerned about his baldness. He constantly attempts to brush his thin strands of hair forward. He has a large growth of hair in his ears and nose. He flaunts himself in front of any woman willing to listen to his chicken stories. He regards himself as God's answer to all women; he falls in love with every woman he comes in contact with, and he has an answer for everything and everyone.

His poorly dressed stature is accentuated by a trailing large woollen scarf dotted with large eggs – never seen off of his neck – and a long oversized leather coat, with a fur collar. All of which he apparently wears throughout the year.

And then, there's Gitta.

Ah, yes, Gitta! Married three times. All dead!

She's extremely tall, thin, attractive-looking in a sexy way, with drooping eyes, in her late 80s, with a deep, loud voice, and a high-pitched laugh. She always wears a T-shirt inscribed with the letters "WOPT". Gitta, you see, is a formidable poker player. In her younger days, it has been said she met all three of her deceased husbands at the World Oilman's Poker Tournament.

Generations ago, her family made the voyage, more like an expedition if you ask me, from Pest in Hungary to Little Pletzl. Gitta never ceased telling anyone, now of a diminishing group who would listen, that the men in her family joined as volunteers in the Pest National Guard to fight the Croatians.

Gitta, over the years, somehow had acquired a pseudo-Hungarian accent, the likes of which in Little Pletzl remained exclusively with her.

She never acknowledged Abe, much to his

irritation. After all, Abe was only a village chicken farmer, and her family came from Pest!

The third member was none other than Zemel's Bakery assistant manager, Yossel, who constantly bellowed at everyone. In his youth, he had dreamed of being a poet. Not just an ordinary poet, but also a writer of satirical prose. He revered Heinrich Heine, a distant cousin of Karl Marx.

However, Yossel's one major failure can be attributed to a prose he wrote about an older man taking a young wife. It commenced, "When an old man takes a young wife, he becomes young and she old."

Needless to say, there was an uproar! The president of The Little Pletzl Council of Women (LPCW), none other than Gitta, came out strongly against Yossel's attempted prose, even though he, with every bit of clarity he could muster, declared his work was satirical in nature and by no means offensive to women.

As expected, the name of Yossel was affirmed by the LPCW as being persona non grata, and he was subsequently banned forthwith from attending all of the Little Pletzl literary events. Such was the power of the LPCW.

The point is, from then on, dejected and full of remorse, Yossel never wrote again. But instead, he took up finger painting.

The final member of this colourful troupe was the extraordinaire accountant and part-time basso profondo opera singer Velvel. Velvel was a huge man, measuring some 200 cm tall and weighing in at 125 kg. For that portly figure of a no-nonsense accountant, the rumour was he was a very distant relative of Velvel Zbarjerin, the famous itinerant singer of yesteryear who died in 1884. Not to confuse you with the two personalities, I will refer to Velvel, my lunch guest from now on, as Velvel from Pletzl.

As to his stature, the similarity couldn't be denied. In his early twenties, Velvel from Pletzl had already established himself as a real folksy poet whose songs about the olden days brought many a tear to his audience as he sang and danced in costume, for anyone who would listen to him in the Shenken, Pletzl's distillery.

However, I can well imagine that you may not believe me as to what I'm about to tell you. Velvel from Pletzl never performed without his whistling kettle always clutched in his right hand while he sang. Not an ordinary whistling kettle, but a top-of-the-line 0.5 L Little Pletzl kettle, with Do, Re, Mi, Fa, Sol, La, and Ti etched on the spout.

One song in particular, *"I love you from afar"*, became a favourite to all the married men quietly having a drink or two away from their wives!

Velvel from Pletzl was, at least by character, a gentle giant. Empathetic comes to mind. But if there was one sensitive issue he couldn't handle, it was a comment about his shoe size, six or 37 European. For no sooner had one expressed a remark about his small feet, one was subjected to an almighty three-hour selection from Wagner's Die Meistersinger von Nürnberg that was, in a trice, pronounced by Velvel from Pletzl as a fitting response.

CHAPTER TWENTY ONE

Hold on to your Memories

To be quite candid about it, my visit to all three villages was, to say the least, quite enlightening. Every individual I came into contact with, I have to admit, their personalities went far beyond the conventional definition of real life. Without a doubt, all could be featured in a book or, as it's been said, cried out to be a character in a movie.

My astonishing encounters are perhaps expressed more eloquently by Dostoevsky, who said: "We sometimes encounter people, even perfect strangers, who begin to interest us at first sight, somehow suddenly, all at once before a word is spoken."

Take for instance, Captain Idris, the 89-year-old legal representative. He knew everything there was to know about 12th-century Welsh law called *Cyfraith Hywel*, but little else. Captain Idris wore the uniform of a WWI Royal Flying Corps pilot, with a leather hat and goggles, the traditional white silk scarf, and a leather jacket. He had a companion named Aelwen, a life-size blow-up doll, dressed to kill, that was attached to the Captain's left foot.

And then there was Penelope, the registered nurse, who yearned to become one of the foremost artists of the European street graffiti period. She had eased into it when she was caught in the act of drawing a graffiti work of Mildred Hastings, the Mayor's wife, sitting on a gold toilet seat. If that wasn't enough to create an impression, she attached it to the exterior wall of The Duke of Wellington pub, facing the village pond. In due course, Penelope was charged and put on probation for one year.

How could anyone forget Blodwin, the publican's deceased young daughter, known to have a fetishism towards malt vinegar? On one of her daily afternoon walks, her nose started sniffing, and with the sun shining directly on her face and her respiratory allergies acting up, she whiffed the malt vinegar lying on top of some French fries, sending her into a tizzy! Regrettably, within fifteen metres of reaching her target, she slipped on some Canada Geese poop, fell into the water, hit her head on a stone, and drowned.

I am reminded of the sheep-shearing thespian twins, Fannie and Hattie Fahey-Fizzard. At the ripe age of 97 years, they are the last of their dynasty. Neither of them married. Now, sadly suffering from acute spectrophobia, they preferred these days to take their place every Monday and Friday, at the Welcome Restaurant & Tea Rooms, sipping on their green tea amongst regular patrons, quietly acknowledging with a smile and a twinkle in their eyes anyone who recognised them. Very few did!

I recall meeting the delightful Chef Violet White-Walsh and hearing about her Mudders Maundy Thursday Baked Mug Cakes, the ones ordered for Good Friday, but all eaten by Dr Piddy Adfat's drunken peacocks and peahens.

I was honoured to attend The Little Figgy Music Ensemble's final rehearsal, where under the direction of their musical director, composer, and arranger hymnodist Delbert Brown, two outstanding newly created pieces of music, *Love is Sweet, but it's Tastier with a Piece of Fish* and *I'm a Son of a Sea Cook*, were presented at the annual Little Figgy Hootie Music Festival.

And finally, it was my friend our Father John Murphy, who invited me to join him at the annual commemoration service of St. Fiacre, the patron saint for haemorrhoid sufferers, at his church, The Gates of Heaven Help Us.

It was, as they say, a fitting end to a memorable visit.

ABOUT THE AUTHOR

Alan L. Simons is a Canadian author, writer, and social & allyship advocate. He was born and educated in London, England. As a diplomat, he served as the Honorary Consul of the Republic of Rwanda to Canada in the post-genocide era. He lectures and writes on issues relating to religion in politics, antisemitism, intolerance, hate, Islamofascism, conflict, and terrorism. *An Anthology of Witty & Oddball Village Stories* is his eighth published book.

alanlsimons.com

EIGHTEEN MONTHS-A LOVE STORY INTERRUPTED

A story of a human relationship that testifies to the strength and will of both the terminally ill patient and her partner as he comes to accept her illness and the short period of time they will spend together.

THE VILLAGE OF LITTLE COMELY-ON-THE-MARSH

This hilarious and satirical story weaves around the lives of an eccentric Welsh community living in a small village somewhere in southeastern France, exclusively in their own sheltered world.

THE VILLAGE OF LITTLE PLETZL-ON-THE-ZUMP

The Village of Little Pletzl-on-the-Zump weaves around the lives of a bizarre Yiddish-speaking community of 613 people living for hundreds of years in a small village also in southeastern France. They speak a unique dialect called Frantsoydish.

THE VILLAGE OF LITTLE FIGGY-ON-THE-DUFF

The Village of Little Figgy-on-the-Duff, the final book in the Village Trilogy, is an eclectic and wonderfully engaging story about what happens to a homogeneous community of Newfoundlanders and Labradorians, whose ancestors originally fled their homeland because of a fear the Vikings would make them wear traditional Norse clothing and take over the dry salt cod industry.

THE CHILDREN OF THE FOREST

Written for both grown-ups and older children, the book is loosely based on a story by Rabbi Nahman of Bratslav. It is a folktale in the European tradition. Kabbalistic, Mystical, Esoteric, and Freygish. It is an account of two Polish Jewish children from pre-teens to adulthood, together with five mystical characters and Klezmer musicians.

THE INCREDIBLE ADVENTURES OF CAPTAIN MACDUDDYFUNK IN CUGGERMUGGERLAND

The children of Canada's Minister of Missing Islands are magically transported to the mysterious island of Cuggermuggerland, where they meet the Quidnuncs, who love to hug, and the Shilpits, who always scream and shout at each other. Captain MacDuddyfunk escorts the two children through a series of exciting adventures, culminating in Allison and Richard showing the Quidnuncs and the Shilpits that two diverse communities can come together to live in harmony.

SWEATY CATS AND BABY PIGEONS

Eight short stories are written for the inquiring mind of a young child, with the view that grandparents play an important role in the development of their little loved ones. Many grandparents have had to accept that their grandchildren do not live around the corner from them. Therefore, intensive periods of involvement with them are relatively short. Yet, we still strive at every opportunity to keep in touch with our grandchildren.

"I grew up in a village of 12 houses. We had a well and a cow."

-Olesya Rulin

https://baronelbooks.com
baronelbooks@protonmail.com

https://alanlsimons.com

https://anthologystories.me
anthologystories@proton.me